THE CHRISTMAS BABY

For all the world's babies
and for my own sweet babe
—M. D. B.

Come let us adore Him, Christ the Lord
—R. C.

SIMON & SCHUSTER BOOKS FOR YOUNG READERS • An imprint of Simon & Schuster Children's Publishing Division • 1230 Avenue of the Americas, New York, New York 10020 • Text copyright © 2009 by Marion Dane Bauer • Illustrations copyright © 2009 by Richard Cowdrey • All rights reserved, including the right of reproduction in whole or in part in any form. • SIMON & SCHUSTER BOOKS FOR YOUNG READERS is a trademark of Simon & Schuster, Inc. • Book design by Laurent Linn • The text for this book is set in Brioso Pro. • The illustrations for this book are rendered with acrylics on illustration board. • Manufactured in China • 10 9 8 7 6 5 4 3 2 • Library of Congress Cataloging-in-Publication Data • Bauer, Marion Dane. • The Christmas baby / Marion Dane Bauer ; illustrated by Richard Cowdrey. • p. cm. • Summary: A simple retelling of the Nativity story that celebrates the timeless joy of welcoming a new baby into the world. • ISBN: 978-1-4169-7885-5 (hardcover) • 1. Jesus Christ—Nativity—Juvenile fiction. [1. Jesus Christ—Nativity—Fiction. 2. Babies—Fiction.] I. Cowdrey, Richard, ill. II. Title. PZ7.B3262Hav 2009 [E]—dc22 2008022930

THE CHRISTMAS BABY

MARION DANE BAUER

illustrated by RICHARD COWDREY

SIMON & SCHUSTER BOOKS FOR YOUNG READERS

NEW YORK   LONDON   TORONTO   SYDNEY

Long, long ago
in a faraway country
in a tiny town,
a man knocked on a door.

"Have you heard?" he called.
"A baby!
A baby is coming!"
"No room here," the innkeeper said,
and he shut the door.

The man knocked again
and again
and again.
"Have you heard?" he cried.
"A baby!
A baby is coming soon."

"No room here!
No room here!"
the innkeepers each replied.
And they shut their doors,
one
after
another.

The man stood as still as stone,
a hand on the neck of the donkey
that had carried his wife
into this land of strangers.
"Have you heard?" he whispered to the donkey.
"A baby is coming this very night!"

The donkey twitched her ears,
nodded her head,
and led her master to a stable
filled with beasts
and with fragrant hay.

"Have you heard?" the man asked the beasts.
"We have heard," they answered.
"We have been waiting.
Come in."

When the baby was born
the beasts shouted with joy.
"Have you heard?" they whinnied
and brayed and mooed
and barked and bleated.
"He is come!"

Angels sang too,
in their satin voices.
And the stars joined in as well.
"Have you heard?
Have you heard?
He is here!"

Shepherds heard.
They left their flocks in the fields
and searched out the stable
so they could admire the baby.

Kings heard.
They left their kingdoms
and journeyed far and far
to bring gifts for the baby.

Mary and Joseph received them all,
beasts and shepherds,
angels and kings.
"Give thanks with us," they said to each one.
"God has given us a baby."

And the baby,
the dear baby,
lay in his bed of fragrant hay
and smiled at the world
with God's own smile.

Now . . . every time a baby is born,
stars and angels sing
in their satin voices.
"Have you heard?
Have you heard?"

Mamas and daddies
and grandmas and grandpas
and aunts and uncles
and cousins and friends,
travel far and far
bringing gifts.

"Have you heard?"
they say to one another.
"A baby!
Our baby is here!"

And you—
when that dear little baby was you—
do you know what you did?

Yes . . . of course.
You smiled back at us all
with
God's
own
smile!